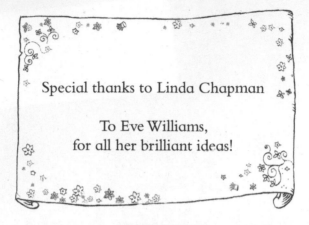

Special thanks to Linda Chapman

To Eve Williams,
for all her brilliant ideas!

ORCHARD BOOKS

First published in Great Britain in 2014 by Orchard Books
This edition published in 2017 by The Watts Publishing Group

5 7 9 10 8 6 4

© 2014 Hothouse Fiction Limited
Illustrations © Orchard Books 2014

A CIP catalogue record for this book is available from the British Library.

ISBN 978 1 40832 918 4

Printed in Great Britain by Clays Ltd, St Ives plc

MIX
Paper from
responsible sources
FSC
www.fsc.org
FSC® C104740

The paper and board used in this book are made from wood from responsible sources

Orchard Books
An imprint of Hachette Children's Group
Part of The Watts Publishing Group Limited
Carmelite House, 50 Victoria Embankment, London EC4Y 0DZ

An Hachette UK Company
www.hachette.co.uk
www.hachettechildrens.co.uk

Series created by Hothouse Fiction
www.hothousefiction.com

# Starlight Adventure

## ROSIE BANKS

# This is the Secret Kingdom

# Starshine Manor

# Book
# One

# Contents

# A Shining Light

Smoke drifted up from the fire. Jasmine watched the flames dance and grinned. The marshmallow on the end of her stick was starting to melt and go crispy on the outside. Even though she had just eaten three hot dogs, her tummy rumbled. She loved toasted marshmallows!

*In fact,* Jasmine thought happily, *this is the perfect evening!* She was sitting in her pyjamas around a campfire with her two best friends, Summer and Ellie, and Summer's family. She snuggled deeper into the fluffy fleece she was wearing over her pyjamas. The autumn air felt slightly cold and damp and leaves lay on the ground, but she knew their cosy tent and sleeping bags would keep them toasty warm when they went to bed.

"I think the marshmallows are done," said Ellie, pulling hers away from the fire.

Jasmine nibbled a corner of oozy marshmallow. It was sweet and sticky and completely delicious. "Yum!" she said with a grin.

"Careful, Finn," Summer warned one of her little brothers who was sitting nearby.

"Your marshmallow is going to melt completely!"

But it was too late. The marshmallow at the end of Finn's stick was already dripping gloopily on to the ground.

"It looks like a mutant marshmallow," said Connor, Summer's other little brother, inspecting it.

"It's the mutant marshmallow of doom!" said Finn in a spooky voice, waving it around on the stick. "Anyone it touches will turn into a marshmallow zombie." He gave an evil laugh.

"Attack!" said Connor. The two little boys started pretend-fighting with their marshmallowy sticks.

The girls squealed and hastily jumped out of the way as sticky marshmallow blobs flew all around them.

"Finn! Connor!" called Mrs Hammond, looking over from where she was sitting with Summer's stepdad, Mike. "That's enough of that. Sit down."

The boys stopped fighting.

"Maybe it's time for some music," said Mike. He picked up his guitar and started to strum a cheerful tune.

"I love this song," said Jasmine happily. Part of her wanted to get up and dance, but she couldn't bring herself to leave her warm spot by the fire, so instead she just shut her eyes and began to imagine herself twirling in the firelight.

Ellie took a notebook out of her fleece pocket and started to sketch a picture of them all sitting in front of their tent.

Summer looked into the trees and thought about all the nocturnal animals who would be waking up about now — badgers, hedgehogs, foxes. She wondered if any of them would wander out of the trees. She loved all animals — big and small. It was so exciting to be there in the woods, surrounded by them all.

Just then, Finn and Connor started play-fighting again, picking bits of melted marshmallow off the ground and throwing them at each other.

"Time for bed, I think," said Mrs Hammond hastily, standing up. "Come on, boys. I'll take you to the shower block to brush your teeth, then you can have a story in your tent."

She herded them away.

"Peace at last!" Summer sighed happily,

lying back on the rug as Mike carried on playing. The stars twinkled overhead and the music filled the air.

Ellie and Jasmine flopped beside her and they all looked up at the stars.

"Isn't this perfect?" Jasmine said.

Ellie rolled on to her tummy. "You know what would make it even better?" She dropped her voice so only Jasmine and Summer could hear. "A visit to the Secret Kingdom!"

The girls smiled at each other. The Secret Kingdom was an incredible, magical world that only they knew about. Whenever there was trouble in the land, the kind ruler, King Merry, sent the girls a message in the Magic Box they looked after. The girls had been there lots of times and had had all sorts of adventures with mermaids, pixies, elves and other amazing creatures.

"Oh, I wish we could go to the Secret Kingdom tonight," whispered Summer. She checked to make sure that her stepdad wasn't listening, but he was still busy playing his guitar. "But I guess they won't need our help now that nasty Queen Malice doesn't have her magic anymore."

Queen Malice was King Merry's horrid sister. She was always inventing wicked plans to try to become the ruler of the Secret Kingdom, but the last time the girls had been there they had defeated her and she had lost all her magic.

"Sometimes King Merry sends for us even when the kingdom *isn't* in trouble," Jasmine reminded Summer and Ellie. "Like when he asked us to join him on his summer holiday to watch the Dolphin Dances, or that time he asked us to Christmas Castle to meet Santa." She frowned. "Although even then Queen Malice has always tried to spoil everything by doing something mean."

Ellie sighed longingly. "Wouldn't it be brilliant if we could get an invitation to a Secret Kingdom party or celebration tonight?"

"Why don't we check the Magic Box just in case?" whispered Summer. "It's in my rucksack."

Mike smiled at the girls as they headed into their tent, then he started playing

another song and humming along. The girls' tent had a big bedroom where all their sleeping bags were laid out and a living space where all their clothes and bags were piled up in a heap. Summer found her rucksack and carefully brought out the Magic Box.

It was a beautiful wooden box, with pictures of all kinds of magical creatures on its carved sides and a mirror set into the lid. Not long ago, when Queen Malice had been in charge of the kingdom for a little while, the mirror had become dull and dark. After the girls had helped to defeat her, the mirror became shiny and silver again.

The girls looked at it eagerly now, but it wasn't sparkling and glowing like it did when King Merry or his royal pixie, Trixibelle, sent them a magic message.

Summer
swallowed her
disappointment.
"Oh well,"
she said. "I'm
sure we'll hear
from them
soon."

It probably
had been too much
to hope for that there
would be a message from the Secret
Kingdom just when they were on holiday
and all together, wanting an adventure.
Summer ran her fingers gently over
the gems surrounding the mirror, then
opened the lid.

Inside, the box was divided into six
little compartments. Until recently, each

compartment had been filled with its own magical object, but after their last adventure there were just three things left – a map, a bag of glitter dust and a shining jewel.

Shutting the box, Summer was just about to put it back in her bag when a glowing light flashed across the lid. The girls exchanged excited looks.

The six green jewels on the lid suddenly started to sparkle with light, like stars in the sky. The light spread through the whole box until every inch of it was glowing and shining. Summer caught her breath as she saw curly letters appearing in surface of the mirror.

"There *is* a message for us after all!"

Golden writing swirled across the mirror, forming a rhyme.

They all leaned forward, their hearts beating fast. What was the message going to say?

# Off to the Secret Kingdom!

Ellie read the riddle out loud:

"Look for a house with a dome that
shines bright,
Helping the stars as they shoot
through the night."

As she read the last word, the box's lid
opened again and the map of the Secret
Kingdom floated out of its compartment,
unfolding itself in the air before settling
on the floor between the girls.

"Where is the riddle talking about?" asked Summer.

"It sounds like we've got to find a house with a domed roof," said Jasmine.

"A dome that shines," added Ellie, looking down at the map. It was like looking at the Secret Kingdom through a window – the golden flags on the turrets of King Merry's Enchanted Palace were waving in the breeze and the girls could see the elf butlers hurrying in and out of the palace doors. There were book brownies tending the trees in Fairytale Forest and dream dragons snoozing among the blossom in Dream Dale. There were so many different things to look at that it was impossible to take it all in at once. Even though the girls had visited the Secret Kingdom many times before,

they were always discovering amazing new places! But where was the house the riddle mentioned?

"Here!" said Jasmine suddenly. "What about this?" She pointed to a grand manor house on a hill. It had large glass windows and a huge front door. On the top of the roof was a big glass dome. "It's got a dome, although it isn't shining."

Ellie read out the name written beside
the house. "Starshine Manor. Hmm.
It sounds like the right kind of place.
Maybe the dome doesn't shine all the
time."

"Let's try it!" Summer said excitedly.
She touched the gems on the box's lid
and Jasmine and Ellie did the same.

"Starshine Manor!" they whispered.

There was a bright flash of silver light

and suddenly a tiny star appeared and
whizzed about the tent, circling the
girls' heads before stopping in between
them, right by their
noses. There was a
faint pop and the
star magically
transformed into
a flat leaf, with a
tiny pixie sitting
cross-legged on
top of it.

"Hello, girls!"
the pixie cried
in delight,
jumping
to her feet.
She had messy
blonde hair and

enormous blue eyes, and she was wearing
a long white dress.

"Trixi!" they all cried.

"I'm so glad you got the message!"
Trixi said.

Ellie suddenly felt anxious. "Is there
anything wrong in the Secret Kingdom?"

Trixi laughed. "Oh no. Don't worry

about that. Queen Malice still can't do any magic. King Merry just thought you might like to come and join us for the Starlight Ceremony. It starts tonight at midnight! I'm sure you'll love it!"

Summer felt excitement fizz up inside her — an invitation to visit the Secret Kingdom just for fun! It was exactly what they had wanted. A thought struck her. "Is it a grand ceremony?" she asked, looking down at her clothes. All the girls were wearing their pyjamas with warm jumpers over the top.

"We might need to get dressed."

"You're all dressed perfectly
for the Starlight
Ceremony!" said
Trixi with a giggle.
"Everyone wears
their pyjamas!"
She did a little
spin on her leaf
and the girls
realised that Trixi's
dress was actually
a pretty white
nightdress!

"So, what happens at this
ceremony?" asked Jasmine.

Trixi grinned. "You'll find that out
when we get there! Hold hands!"

The girls grabbed each other's hands.

This was it! They were going to the Secret Kingdom again!

Trixi tapped the ring on her finger and it glowed with a green light. "Starshine Manor!" she called in her tinkly voice.

Green-and-silver sparkles burst out of the ring and swirled around the girls, lifting them up into the air and spinning

them away. Round and round they spun until they started to slow and were set down gently on the ground.

Jasmine looked around and saw that they were standing in a grand hall. The ceiling was high and painted to look like the night sky. A chandelier covered with star-shaped crystals lit the room and the huge windows let in a view of the real starry sky outside. In a corner of the room, a spiral staircase led up to a round hole in the ceiling, just big enough for a person to get through, and at one end of the room there were tables decorated

with long, pretty
star-patterned tablecloths.
The entire floor of the hall
was covered with soft pillows
and brightly coloured sleeping
bags. Some were spotty,
some were stripy, some were
embroidered with pictures of

unicorns and others were covered with sequinned fairies and flowers.

Jasmine put her hand up to her hair and grinned as she felt her tiara settle there. Whenever they arrived in the Secret Kingdom their beautiful tiaras appeared on their heads to show everyone that they were Very Important Friends of kind King Merry.

"This is Starshine Manor, where the Starlight Ceremony happens," said Trixi, zooming happily around their heads on her leaf. "King Merry has a big sleepover party here once a year, on the two nights when all the shooting stars pass over the Secret Kingdom. Look!" She flew to one of the high windows and beckoned to them. They hurried to join her. Through the window they saw a tall pedestal with

an ornate golden
lantern standing on
it. Lots of tartan
blankets had been
spread out on the
lawn nearby.

"Starlight Manor is the only place in the kingdom that you can see the shooting stars from," Trixi explained. "For two nights a year, the stars fly over the kingdom – and if you stand on that very spot..." she smiled, pointing to the lawn outside, "something amazing happens..."

"What?" Summer gasped.

Trixi grinned happily. "Every year, people from all round the kingdom gather to stand out on the lawn and make a wish. At around midnight, when the shooting stars reach the highest point in the sky, they choose a wish and make it come true!"

"So there's only one lucky person?" asked Summer, puzzled. "How do the stars decide which wish to grant?"

"Oh, no," explained Trixi with a

tinkling laugh.
"There are *lots*
of shooting
stars, and they
each grant
a different
wish!"

The girls
exchanged
excited looks.
*A Starlight
Ceremony with
wishing stars – what could be better?*

Just then one of the doors opened
and a small figure came in, surrounded
by elves, pixies and brownies. He was
wearing purple pyjamas, golden slippers
with curly toes and a purple dressing
gown embroidered with crowns. A golden

crown was perched on top of his long
sleeping cap.

"King Merry!" cried the girls happily,
running over to him.

"Hello, dear friends!" the king
exclaimed, beaming at them. "Oh, stars
and moons! How simply wonderful it is

to see you. I hope you're prepared for a night of wishes and fun that you will never forget!"

# Summer's Story

The doors opened again and more elves, pixies and brownies came hurrying into the room with plates of food and jugs of drink. There were star-shaped biscuits, cupcakes that looked like planets and little sandwiches cut into crescent-shaped moons. It all looked delicious!

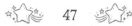

"This is the midnight feast!" Trixi told the girls as it was laid out on the tables. "We always eat it now while we're trying to stay awake, waiting for midnight to come."

Jasmine grinned. "We always eat our midnight feasts early when *we're* having a sleepover too."

"We try to wait until midnight," Ellie giggled, "but we never can!"

The elves and brownies and pixies all greeted the girls and jumped into their sleeping bags, chatting and laughing. It was like the biggest sleepover ever!

"It's lovely here, King Merry," said Summer. "Thank you for inviting us."

"We were worried Queen Malice might be causing trouble again when we saw the message," admitted Ellie.

The king chuckled. "Oh dearie me, no," he said. "Thankfully, my sister can't do much without her magic. She did cause a bit of a fuss recently when she and her horrible Storm Sprites tried to steal the mermaids' wishing pearl, but without her magic the mermaids easily stopped her." He shook his head, making the bobble at the end of his nightcap bounce around.

"You needn't worry about her at all tonight. Not at all."

Summer and Ellie smiled back at him but Jasmine frowned slightly. She didn't trust Queen Malice. There had been times in the past when King Merry had thought his sister had changed, but she had always come up with another wicked plan. Jasmine hoped it would be different this time.

"So, my dears, have you seen the magic lantern in the garden?" King Merry asked them.

"Yes, we saw it through the window," said Jasmine, glancing outside.

"What's it for?" Summer asked curiously.

"And why is the lid open?" added Ellie.

"It collects starlight all year long," King

Merry explained. "When it's full to the brim, the lid closes. Then we take it up to the observatory. It sends a beam of starlight out into the sky which guides all the shooting stars over the lawn to grant wishes." He clapped his hands in delight. "It is quite a wonderful sight to behold!"

Summer noticed one of the elf butlers coming over.

"Your Majesty!" he said. "The lantern is now full and ready for the ceremony. Would you like us to bring it in here?"

The king did an excited jig on the spot. "Oh, yes please! Let's have it in here with us. Now, dear friends, do come and sit down. Over here! This way!"

He led the way over to a fancy royal-purple sleeping bag covered with golden crown-shaped cushions, with a floaty purple canopy overhead. When they got there, Trixi tapped her pixie ring and three more sleeping bags appeared next to it – Summer's was sunshine yellow, Jasmine's was bright pink and Ellie's was green with purple spots on.

"Thanks, Trixi!" the girls grinned as they snuggled down into the squishy softness of their sleeping bags.

The elf butler reappeared, carefully carrying the lantern. Everyone in the room stopped talking and watched as the butler carried it over to the spiral staircase and put it down gently, then stepped back. Silver light shone out, illuminating the whole hall in a beautiful, sparkly glow.

"It's so pretty," breathed Summer.

"And so magical," agreed King Merry. "Now everyone, it's time to let the midnight feast begin!"

Everyone jumped up and started helping themselves to food and drink.

"And I've just got comfy!" Jasmine sighed, shifting on her sleeping bag as she prepared to stand up.

Trixi grinned. "Don't worry. I can help

with that." She tapped her pixie ring and each of the girls found a cake stand beside them filled with a selection of the delicious cookies, cakes and sandwiches. King Merry had his own royal cake stand, and Trixie had a tiny one to balance on her leaf.

"Oh, well done, Trixi!" the king said.

"Tuck in, everyone!"

They all started to eat. For a while there was silence in the hall as everyone enjoyed the yummy food.

King Merry finally sat back on his sleeping bag and gave a huge yawn. "That was delicious, but now I don't know how I will stop myself from falling asleep! And the stars won't be at their highest for a little while yet."

Around him, several of the elves and brownies were starting to yawn too.

"We mustn't fall asleep!" Trixi said in alarm. "It would be awful if we missed the ceremony. No one would be able to have any wishes this year! There must be some way of staying awake."

"Maybe we could have a dance?" suggested Jasmine hopefully.

The king groaned and patted his tummy. "Not at the moment. I feel like I might pop!"

"I know!" Trixi said suddenly. "You girls were really good at telling stories when we had that adventure in Fairytale Forest. Maybe you could tell us all an exciting story now – one that would keep us all awake."

"Oh, yes!" King Merry's glasses jumped on his nose as he nodded enthusiastically. "An action-packed story. One so exciting that we couldn't possibly fall asleep! That's a wonderful idea!"

"Summer's brilliant at making up stories," said Ellie. "Can you think of a good one, Summer?"

Everyone looked expectantly at Summer. She blushed. She didn't really

like talking in front of lots of people.
"I…I suppose I could," she faltered.

Jasmine squeezed her hand. "You'll be
great. Ellie and I will help you if you run
out of ideas."

Ellie nodded and Summer gave them
a grateful look. She knew she could
manage it with her best friends helping.
"OK…well, I'm sure I can think of

something…" Her mind turned over
quickly. What could the story be about?
Maybe something scary? That would
keep everyone awake. She thought of
what her brothers had been doing around
the campfire and that gave her an idea.
"OK!" she said again. "I've thought of
something."

All the elves and
brownies got into
their sleeping
bags and
cuddled up in
a big circle.
King Merry
snuggled down
in his sleeping
bag and Trixi
perched her leaf

next to him. The starshine lantern cast
a twinkling light over everyone as they
listened, waiting for the story to begin.

"It was a cold, dark night in the Secret
Kingdom," Summer started off. "All the
trees in Monster Forest were covered
with frost. No one in the Secret Kingdom
usually went into Monster
Forest because
it was far too
scary, but
one night a
brave little
pixie,
Trixi,
knew she
had to go
in there
because she

was on a mission for King Merry!"

The king chortled in delight. Trixi blushed and hid her face in her hands.

"Trixi flew deep into the forest," Summer went on. "She thought she caught sight of some horrible creatures lurking in the shadows, but she ignored them and kept going…" She paused.

"Go on!" breathed King Merry. Trixi and all the other elves, brownies and pixies were hanging on her every word.

Summer forgot to be shy as she looked at their excited faces.

"Trixi heard a noise behind her and looked round. It was a bat zombie!"

TAP TAP TAP.

Everyone shrieked as there really was a loud tapping noise from behind them. To Summer's horror, they turned to see

six mean, grey
faces peering in
through one of
the windows. The
creatures had
bat-like wings,
small beady eyes
and were tapping
at the glass with
twiggy fingers.

"AAAAAAGGH!"
Everyone shrieked in fright.

It's the bat zombies!" cried a
frightened little elf.

"But I just made up bat zombies,
they're not real." Summer looked around
nervously and her voice wobbled. "Are
they?"

"No, wait!" shouted Jasmine, jumping

to her feet as she recognised the familiar faces outside. "Those aren't bat zombies! They're Queen Malice's Storm Sprites."

"But what are my sister's Storm Sprites doing here?" cried King Merry, looking very pale.

Cackles of laughter rang out from

outside the window. "What are we doing here?" cried one of the sprites. "We've come to spoil your fun, of course!"

# Tricked!

Everyone screamed as the six Storm
Sprites flew into the hall. Two of them
landed on the tables and jumped up and
down, trampling the food and knocking
over the drinks. Another two pelted the
elves, pixies and brownies with misery
drops that made anyone they hit feel
sad and unhappy. The magical creatures
squealed and yelped as they ducked

and dodged. The last two Storm Sprites started bursting the pillows open with their pointy fingers, sending feathers flying everywhere.

"Stop it, you horrible things! Stop it right now!" cried King Merry, shaking his fist at them, but the Storm Sprites just ignored him.

"We're going to ruin your silly starlight sleepover!" they chanted together gleefully.

"Oh no, you're not!" Jasmine cried, putting her hands on her hips. She ran to the table where two of the sprites were standing and yanked the tablecloth out from under their feet, sending them falling to the ground in a tangle of limbs and wings. The rest of the food tumbled off too and splattered all over them.

"Agh!" one cried, wiping icing away from his eyes.

"You can't stop us!" the other one scowled.

"You want to bet?" said Jasmine, picking up a pillow and bashing him with it.

Ellie joined in, throwing a jug of water at another of the Storm Sprites who was about to throw a misery drop at a little elf. "Take that, you horrible sprite!" she yelled as the water splashed over him.

At the same time, Summer threw a big blanket over one of the sprites who was wrecking the pillows.

He wailed loudly as he thrashed around. "It's gone dark! Where is everyone? Who turned out the lights?"

Starshine Manor was filled with the sound of yelling, bellowing and shouting. But suddenly in the middle of all the chaos Jasmine saw something that made her blood run cold. A tall, thin woman with frizzy black hair was sneaking up the stairs towards the starlight lantern. Jasmine watched, dismayed, as the woman's bony hands reached out for it...

"Queen Malice!" shrieked Jasmine.

"Queen Malice is trying to steal the starshine lantern!"

She shouted the words so loudly that everyone turned to look at the lantern. Queen Malice snatched it up and hugged it to her bony chest.

"I've got the lantern now!" she crowed. "Now the stars won't be guided on their way and no one will have a wish granted this year!"

"Oh really? Well, we'll see about that!" cried Trixi. She tapped her pixie ring.

*"Pixie magic, hear me sing,*
*Lantern fly right to the king!"*

There was a flash of light and the lantern shot out of Queen Malice's hands and headed straight towards King Merry.

Jasmine tensed, waiting for the queen to fight back with her thunderbolt staff. But Queen Malice couldn't, of course. Her magic had gone!

"Gah!" the queen shouted, stamping her foot as the lantern flew away.

"Oh, well done, Trixi!" Ellie cried as the lantern landed safely in the little king's arms.

"Oh no, you don't!" Jasmine said fiercely as one of the sprites flew towards the king, its spiky fingers outstretched. "Quick, everyone, gather round King Merry," she yelled, stepping in front of him protectively.

The girls, elves, brownies and pixies all surrounded him.

"If you want that lantern, you're going to have to get through us!" Ellie cheered.

The Storm Sprites pushed and shoved, but everyone stood firm.

"You can't stop us!" called King Merry triumphantly. "The lantern is going up to the observatory where it belongs! Come on, everyone! Let's take it there before the

shooting stars reach their highest point in the sky. We have to guide them over Starshine Manor, or no one will be able to make any wishes."

All the pixies, elves and brownies stayed in a tight circle around the king as he carried the lantern towards the staircase.

"Sprites! Stop them!" Queen Malice screeched angrily.

But the sprites couldn't. The crowd around King Merry just wouldn't let them through, no matter how much they scrabbled and fought. King Merry climbed the spiral staircase with the lantern in his arms. Everyone else followed him. They all climbed through the entrance hatch in the ceiling and came out in a beautiful glass observatory with a domed roof made of lots of curved panes of glass. The stars twinkled in the night sky above them.

The king carried the lantern carefully over to a golden pedestal right in the centre of the observatory.

"Crowns and sceptres, we did it!" he declared as he placed the lantern down.

"And only just in time!"

Everyone gasped as they heard a clock in a nearby tower starting to chime midnight.

"Let the Starlight Ceremony begin!"

King Merry opened the lantern and
a beam of beautiful silver starlight burst
out, filling the glass dome, then flowing
through an open window out into the
clear night sky.

The girls and the pixies, brownies and elves all whooped and Trixi turned a loop the loop in excitement.

"Look! The stars are coming now!"

In the distance, hundreds of shooting stars started streaking across the sky like fireworks, guided safely across the kingdom by the lantern's light.

King Merry hugged the girls. "We beat my sister! Thank goodness she doesn't have her magic. We managed to stop her and she didn't ruin the day!"

"Oh, didn't I?" Through the window came a shriek of wild laughter from the lawn below. They saw Queen Malice standing down on the grass, looking up at them with a nasty smug expression on her face.

"What's she doing?" said Jasmine, opening another window to peer down at the wicked queen.

"Oh, brother, you can be so very foolish at times!" Queen Malice crowed. "This is *exactly* what I wanted to happen. Now I'll be the only one on the lawn when the stars fly overhead. And if I'm the only one there, *my* wish is sure to be granted!"

Ellie, Jasmine and Summer looked at each other in horror.

"Oh no!" gasped Summer in dismay. "It was all a trick!"

Jasmine started running towards the
hole in the floor where the staircase was,
but before she could reach it, the hatch
door slammed shut.

She tried to pull it open but it was
locked from the other side. She could
hear the Storm Sprites cackling with
laughter.

"You can't get out! Queen Malice will
get her wish!" they screeched.

"Oh dearie me, this is dreadful!"
groaned King Merry. "We have to get
down onto the lawn or none of us will be
able to make our wishes!"

Just then, the queen threw her head
back and reached her scrawny arms up
towards the sky. "I wish to have all my
magic back and be even more powerful
than I was before!"

One by one, stars started to shoot past, high overhead. Ellie gasped. She'd never seen a shooting star before. They were so beautiful. And Queen Malice was going to use them to grant her horrid wish!

"Do it!" shrieked the queen. "I want my magic NOW!"

"Trixi! Quick!" Ellie said. "Can you use your magic to send us down to the lawn before her wish is granted?"

"Yes of course! Um…" Trixi started. *"Pixie magic—"*

"It's too late!" gasped Summer. "Look!"

A silvery light had surrounded Queen Malice. She seemed to glow and sparkle

as starlight surrounded her. "At last!" she cried, her eyes glittering with triumph. "My magic has returned!"

# Dark Magic

Summer grabbed Ellie and Jasmine's hands as they watched from the observatory. Finally, the light faded, leaving Queen Malice standing tall and gloating in the garden.

"Thunder staff, appear!" the horrid queen commanded.

A huge black staff with a large golden thunderbolt at the top appeared in her right hand. It was even bigger than her old staff and the thunderbolt was spikier.

Queen Malice swept it up and pointed it at the sky.

"Cast down stars that shine so bright,
Dark and dull now be the night!
Now that my own wish is done,
No more wishing for anyone!"

There was a loud clap of thunder and suddenly all the stars disappeared. The sky was completely black, lit only by a thin crescent moon.

"What are you doing, sister?" King Merry cried, pounding on the glass dome of the observatory.

"Making you pay!" Queen Malice gave a gleeful laugh. "Now I have my magic back I will make everyone miserable, and there's nothing you can do to stop me!" She pointed her staff at the sky again and this time there was a flash of lightning and a thundercloud appeared. Queen Malice jumped onto it. "A good night's work, my sprites," she crowed.

"I have my magic back, and the stars will never light up the skies again!"

Cackling with delight, the Storm Sprites leaped away from the staircase hatch and flew out into the garden to join the queen. They turned in the air and pulled faces at the watching crowd.

"We told you Queen Malice would win!" they taunted.

"To Thunder Castle!" the queen screamed and the black thundercloud sped away, with the Storm Sprites flapping alongside it.

King Merry's shoulders slumped. "What are we going to do? All the beautiful stars have gone."

"And now there's no wishing magic for anyone else," Trixi said sadly.

"We stopped Queen Malice taking the

lantern – but what she did was much worse," Summer said, looking at where the stars used to be.

All around, the elves, pixies and brownies started panicking as they looked up at the empty sky.

"We have to fix this!" Jasmine said.

"But what can we do?" sighed Trixi.

"Queen Malice said, 'Cast down stars'," Ellie said thoughtfully.

"Like they've fallen out of the sky," Jasmine agreed.

"So they must be in the kingdom somewhere, just not in the sky where they're supposed to be!" Summer finished.

"Oh, girls, I don't know what we'd do without you," King Merry said. "Trixi, send a message round – get everyone to search for any trace of the stars. Maybe once we've found them we can work out how to get them back into the sky."

"And get their wishing magic back!" Ellie added.

"There's still plenty of light left in the lantern. And there's one more chance for everyone to make their wishes tomorrow night." Summer added hopefully.

"I'll send a glow-worm message," Trixi said, tapping her pixie ring. "They'll tell everyone in the kingdom to look out for the falling stars and let us know if they find one."

Jasmine looked up at the black sky and sighed. All over the Secret Kingdom, glow-worms would be waking up, shining brightly and passing the message to everyone who saw them. She felt so helpless, and wished she had a job to do, as well.

"There's nothing we can do now but wait," Trixi said.

Everyone sat down on the blankets and looked up at the night sky. Some got into their sleeping bags, but the excited sleepover mood was gone.

Jasmine, Summer and Ellie linked arms. Despite herself, Summer couldn't help yawning.

Trixi gave a tiny pixie yawn as well. "I think we should all get some sleep," she said. "Girls, why don't I take you home and you can come back tomorrow? We'll keep searching in the meantime, and send you a message as soon as we have news."

Jasmine nodded. She didn't want to leave while the stars were missing, but she couldn't think while her head was so tired. "Please don't worry, everyone," she said, sounding more confident than she felt. "We'll come back tomorrow and we'll break Queen Malice's horrid spell and get the stars back!"

Trixi flew round and kissed each

of them on the nose. "I'll send you a message in the Magic Box tomorrow," she told them. "Make sure you watch out for it."

"We will," Ellie agreed.

"See you tomorrow." Summer promised.

The girls waved to all their friends,

then held hands. Trixi tapped her pixie ring and a cloud of sparkles swept them away. They tumbled over and over before landing back in the tent.

Outside, Mike was still playing his guitar. No time ever passed in the real world while the girls were away in the Secret Kingdom, so thankfully no one ever realised they'd gone.

Jasmine shook her head. "What an awful end to the evening."

Summer picked up the Magic Box, which was still in the middle of the tent. "We have to stop Queen Malice. It's horrible to think of the Secret Kingdom having no stars in the sky."

"It's not just the Secret Kingdom," Ellie gasped as she peered through the flap of the tent. "Come and look outside."

Summer and Jasmine joined Ellie in the tent entrance. Every star in the sky above the campsite had gone.

"Oh no," breathed Summer. "Queen Malice's new magic must be so powerful that her spell has even affected the stars in our world!"

Mike noticed them peering out and looking at the sky. He glanced up too. "Goodness. There were lots of stars last time I looked up," he said. "It must have got cloudy all of a sudden."

But the girls knew Queen Malice was to blame. They went back into the tent miserably.

"We'll sort it out," vowed Jasmine.

Ellie nodded. "We won't let her win."

"No way," said Summer.

The friends swapped determined looks. Even though there were no shooting stars in the sky overhead, they knew they were all making the same, silent wish – to stop

Queen Malice. Tomorrow night they would return to Starshine Manor, but this time they'd be ready for her!

# Starshine Wish

# Contents

# Back to the Secret Kingdom

"Goodness, it's been a busy day," Summer's mum sighed as she sat down in her camping chair by the fire. The sun had just set and, with no stars in the sky, the only light came from the rising moon and the flickering flames of the campfire.

"We've had a great time, Mum," said Summer, going over and giving her a big hug. "Thank you!"

"Yes, thank you so much," Jasmine and Ellie agreed.

That day, they'd been for a long walk in the woods, had a play-fight with the dry leaves, collected conkers, had a delicious barbecue and finished off by eating toffee and drinking hot chocolate by the fire, while Mike, Summer's step-dad, played his guitar again.

It had been lovely, but all day long Summer had been thinking about the Secret Kingdom, and she knew her two best friends felt the same. They'd kept sneaking away to look in the Magic Box, but there was no message from Trixi or King Merry. Summer felt a yawn building up inside her but she swallowed it back down. She and the others couldn't be tired tonight. They had to break

Queen Malice's wicked spell and get all the stars back in the sky!

Summer glanced over to where Jasmine and Ellie were sitting together. *Maybe we should go and check the Magic Box again,* she thought.

Jasmine seemed to be thinking the same thing, because as she caught Summer's eye she gave her and Ellie a meaningful look. Summer nodded.

"I think we might go and get ready for bed, Mum," Summer said quickly. "We'll just go and brush our teeth in the shower block."

"It's very dark," her mum replied. "Will you be OK going on your own?"

"We'll take a torch," Summer said. She turned to the others and winked. "Shall we go now?"

They jumped to their feet.

"Ready when you are!" said Jasmine.

"I've got our toothbrushes and flannels here," said Ellie holding up her rucksack, with the familiar shape of the Magic Box hidden inside.

As they looked at the bag, it started to glow! Summer gasped. It must be a message in the Magic Box!

The three of them hurried away.

As soon as they were out of earshot, Jasmine did an excited pirouette. "We're going to have another adventure!" she said with a grin.

Ellie hugged the rucksack. "Oh, I hope this one has a happy ending and we get the stars back."

"Breaking Queen Malice's spell isn't going to be easy," Summer warned. "And now she has her magic again, she's bound to try and stop us."

"We've beaten her before," said Jasmine. "We'll do it again tonight!"

They reached the shower block and found an empty changing cubicle. After pulling the curtain shut so no one would see them, they took out the Magic Box. Its mirrored lid was shimmering and

shining, lighting up the darkness. Words were swirling up in the lid.

Jasmine read the message out.

*"Dear friends, you know the place to say,
We need you back here, don't delay!"*

The girls put their hands on the six green gems on the box's lid.

"Starshine Manor!" they all called out. Light swirled out of the box lid and surrounded them. They felt themselves being spun away. Round and round they twirled until their feet hit the ground. Then the light cleared and they saw that they were standing on the lawn outside the great hall. The sky was completely black. All the lights in the manor were on and the observatory was still filled with a

twinkling glow from the starshine lantern, but even with the light spilling out, most of the gardens were hidden in the inky darkness.

The girls found their way to the door
and flung it open. In the hall, all the
sleeping bags had been tidied away and
a huge map of the Secret Kingdom had
been pinned up on the wall. It had silvery
star stickers stuck all over it. King Merry,
who had changed out of his pyjamas,
was standing on a table and using a long
stick to point out the different stars to
the creatures gathered around him. There

were elves and brownies in lines, fairies
fluttering their wings, a small army of
pixies hovering on flying leaves, eight
snowy-white flying horses with long
manes and tails that reached the ground
and three big dragons with shimmering
scales and clawed feet.

"It's Huang, Pan and Chi," whispered Summer, looking at the dragons in delight. The girls had met the dream dragons on some of their other adventures.

"And Swift and Snowshine," said Ellie, recognising two of the flying horses.

"But what are they all doing here?" wondered Jasmine.

King Merry nodded solemnly to the girls in greeting as they made their way through the crowd. His kindly face was more serious than they had ever seen it before.

"Trixi!" Ellie sighed with relief when she spotted their pixie friend. "We've been waiting for your message all day."

"I'm sorry!" Trixi replied, shaking her head. "There was no sign of the stars at

all until it started to get dark and they began to shine. The glow-worm message worked! Everyone searched the whole kingdom and came here to tell us where they had found stars." The little pixie flew her leaf over to them, her face anxious. "We thought if  we could collect them up, we might be able to find some way to get their wishing magic back and get them back up into the sky where they belong."

"Good idea," Summer told her.

"We must break my sister's wicked spell!" King Merry declared. "She's made all the shining jewels that light the roads go dark as well so the kingdom is completely black. Under the cover of this darkness, her Storm Sprites have already stolen all the cakes from the Sugarsweet Bakery and every book from Fairytale Forest. They are running riot all across the kingdom, causing damage and destruction

wherever they go. There is no knowing what Malice will do next! We must find

a way to get the stars back into the sky
– a wish is our best chance to put things
right again."

All the watching creatures nodded.

"Trixi," King Merry said, turning to the
pixie, who was hovering beside him. "Will
you explain the plan?"

"Of course, Your Majesty," Trixi said.
"This map shows where all the stars have
fallen." Turning to the flying horses and
dream dragons, she continued, "Please
can you bring them back here where
they will be safe?"

"We will fly as swiftly as we can,"
rumbled Huang, an enormous purple
dream dragon.

Swift, a majestic flying horse, tossed his
mane. "We'll be back as soon as possible."

"Just tell us where you wish us to go,

Trixibelle," Pan, the pink-and-cream
dragon replied.

Trixi flew her leaf
up and pointed to
a star on the map.
"Huang, can
you collect this
star that's near
Glitter Beach?
And Pan, can
you collect
this one here
from Bubble
Volcano? Swift
will you fly to Swan
Palace..."

As she continued, King Merry turned
to the pixies, elves and brownies. "My
friends, we must prepare the hall for

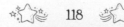

looking after the fallen stars when they are brought back here."

The crowd cleared and King Merry spotted the girls. They ran over to greet him.

"Oh, it's so good to see you, my dears!" said the king happily.

"We came as soon as we got the message in the Magic Box. What can we do?" asked Jasmine.

"I was hoping you could help me look after my guests," said the king.

"Guests?" said Ellie.

King Merry smiled. "Very important ones. Come and see."

They exchanged puzzled looks as they followed him through the crowd, up to the observatory.

"Here they are!" King Merry said, huffing and puffing as he reached the top of the spiral staircase.

The girls stared. The observatory was brighter than ever before. As well as the silvery starlight from the lantern, there was more light shimmering from three large shapes, floating in the middle of the glass dome.

"They're beautiful!" Summer breathed.

King Merry clasped his hands together. "Those, my dear, are fallen stars," he said.

# ⌒The Fallen Stars⌒

"Fallen stars?" echoed Ellie. She, Summer and Jasmine stared at the stars floating in the observatory.

King Merry nodded. "We found these ones in the Starshine Manor gardens."

Ellie went closer. "They're incredible," she breathed.

Suddenly all three stars glowed even brighter and Jasmine, Summer and Ellie gasped as they transformed into girls that

looked about the same age as them. They
floated down until they were standing
on the ground in front of them. One had
dark skin, wavy black hair and almond-
shaped brown eyes, another had a shining
black bob and the third had pale blonde
hair and sky-blue eyes. Their
skin shimmered and
shone as if it was
dusted with
glitter. They
were all so
beautiful
– but they
looked very
sad.

"Hello. I am
Eve, the Evening
Star," the star with

the black bob said to the girls. "And these are my cousins..."

"I'm Nori, the North Star," said the star with the wavy black hair.

"And I'm Morna, the Morning Star," said the star with the blonde hair.

"It's lovely to meet you," said Jasmine, in amazement. She'd never thought she'd get to speak to a star!

"You look just like normal human girls," Ellie said, feeling awe-struck. "Only more sparkly."

Morna smiled. "Stars can take the shape of those we are talking to. If you were unicorns, we would look like unicorns. If you were mermaids, we would look like mermaids. Many people have met a star, they just don't realise it."

"These are my special friends from the

Other Realm – Jasmine, Summer and
Ellie," said King Merry to the stars. "They
have helped stop my sister many times
before when she has caused trouble."

Morna sighed. "I fear you will not be
able to help us this time," she said sadly
and the pale light that glowed from her
skin dimmed.

"Can't you just fly back up into the
sky?" Summer asked gently. "We won't
mind about not having our wishes
granted, as long as you're OK."

Morna sadly shook her head. "No, you
see, shooting stars fly by wishing magic.
Without it, we can barely float and
hover. We'd never reach the highest part
of the sky. Queen Malice's spell brought
us down to the ground by taking our
wishing magic away, and without it we

can't shoot across the sky."

"Worst of all," Nori sobbed, "every shooting star must grant one wish during the Starlight Ceremony. If we don't, we'll lose our magic for good and stay as fallen stars forever."

"Tonight's our last chance!" Morna added. "If we don't return to the sky before dawn, we may never be able to." She looked up at the inky sky sadly, and a shimmering tear rolled down her cheek.

"Oh, my dears, please don't cry," said King Merry, looking distressed. He pulled a spotty handkerchief out of his cloak and handed it to the star. "There, there!"

Morna dabbed her eyes with it. "Thank you, Your Majesty," she whispered.

"It's all my fault," said Eve with a sniff. "I was the star who granted Queen

Malice's wish. Now I'm the only shooting star who can get back into the sky – but I won't go without my friends."

"It's not your fault, cousin," said Nori, hugging her. "You know you had no choice." She turned to the girls to explain. "We listen to all the wishes that are made. When we get to the highest point in the sky, we can use our wishing magic

to make one of them come true."

Nori sighed. "Eve reached the highest point in the sky, and Queen Malice's was the only wish, so she had to grant it."

Eve gave a little sob. "I didn't want to!" she wailed. "If only there had been someone else outside making a wish at the same time, then I could have granted theirs instead."

Just then an elf's head appeared at the top of the staircase. "King Merry! Please, Your Majesty!" He climbed into the observatory and bowed low. "Snowbell the pixie has just found another fallen star in the grounds. The poor star is injured, so we need someone else to help him back to the hall."

Eve gave another sob.

"Oh, dearie me," said the king. "I shall

come and organise someone to help." He hurried away with the elf.

Eve's sobs grew louder.

Summer felt awful. "Please don't be so sad," she said to Eve. "We'll get the fallen star back and help him here."

"It's not that," said Eve through her tears. "I'm sad about the star, but I know he will be well looked after when King Merry gets him back here. It's…well, it's that elf."

They all blinked.

"The elf? What do you mean?" asked Ellie in confusion.

"I don't know," Eve said helplessly. "I just have this feeling – I'm sure it's *his* wish I would have granted if only he'd been outside on the lawn when I flew up to the highest point." She put her head in her hands and cried. "Now his wish won't ever come true!"

The other two stars hugged her.

"We need to find a way to break Queen Malice's spell," said Ellie to Jasmine and Summer. "If we can do that then the stars will get their wishing magic back and will be able to fly up into the sky again."

"And then everyone can make their wishes tonight," said Jasmine.

"But how can we do that?" Morna said, looking at them. "Queen Malice is more powerful than ever now. How can her spell possibly be broken?"

Ellie, Summer and Jasmine looked at each other. Morna was right. What could they do?

# Jasmine's Plan

Jasmine frowned. "OK, let's all think about this. After all, we've broken Queen Malice's horrid spells lots of times before."

Ellie nodded. "Like the time she cast a spell on the pixies' leaves to take away their flying power. The spell broke when we got all the pixies to fly in the air."

"Queen Malice's spell is supposed to stop any wishes being granted..." said Summer thoughtfully.

Jasmine's expression cleared. "So, if we can make a wish come true then the spell might break!"

"But how can we make a wish come true?" asked Ellie.

"I think I've got an idea," said Jasmine. "Where's that elf? The one who didn't get his wish because Queen Malice got it instead?" She looked around. "Is he still with King Merry?"

Ellie went to peer down the spiral staircase. "No, he's over there!" said Ellie, pointing. "Look!"

They all looked down and saw the little elf getting a sleeping bag ready for another star, who looked like a shimmering elf.

"We need to talk to him and find out what his wish was going to be. Maybe

we can make it happen. We'll be back in a moment," Jasmine told the stars.

The girls made their way down the spiral staircase and over towards the young elf.

"Excuse me!" Ellie called out. "Please? Can we have a word with you?"

The little elf looked round in surprise. "Me?" he said.

The girls nodded.

"What's your name?" asked Summer.

"Harrison, miss." He bowed, looking flustered. "I can't believe I'm finally meeting you.

I've heard all about you and how you have helped the Secret Kingdom and King Merry so many times. You must be so brave and clever!"

"Well, we've only managed to stop Queen Malice because other people have helped us," said Jasmine. "And this time we think we need your help."

Harrison looked startled. "Me? What can I do?"

"Were you planning on making a wish last night?" Ellie asked.

The tips of Harrison's pointy ears turned pink. "Um, yes, I was."

"What was it?" Jasmine said eagerly.

The blush spread from Harrison's ears over his face and neck. "Well…um…" He scraped the toe of his boot along the floor and avoided their eyes.

"You can tell us," Summer said softly. "We won't laugh."

"It was such a silly wish," admitted Harrison. "We've got a dance show at school next week and I can't remember the steps. I was…well…I was going to wish that I could do the dance perfectly."

"But that's wonderful!" gasped Jasmine. "That's an easy problem for us to solve!"

Harrison blinked in surprise. "It is?"

"Oh yes!" She grabbed his hands and twirled him round.

"Quick, come with us!"

Harrison hurried back up to the observatory's glass dome with Jasmine, Summer and Ellie. As soon as they got there, Jasmine explained to the stars about Harrison's wish and her plan.

"We think that if we can make Harrison's wish come true then Queen Malice's spell will break!" she finished.

Eve exchanged looks with the other stars. "But we haven't got any wishing magic to grant the wish."

"We don't need magic!" said Jasmine.

Ellie nodded. "Sometimes you can just make wishes come true."

"If you try hard enough," Summer agreed.

"And with a bit of help from your friends," Jasmine added happily.

"Jasmine's a brilliant dancer," Summer explained. "She can help Harrison learn to do it perfectly, just as if his wish had been granted by a shooting star."

The three stars started to shimmer more brightly again.

"That would be wonderful!" cried Morna excitedly.

"But I'm really rubbish at dancing," said Harrison doubtfully.

"Don't worry. Jasmine's an amazing teacher," said Summer. "She's taught me dances before and I bet she'll be able to help you."

Jasmine nodded. "I just need to learn the dance first myself then I can teach you." She frowned. "Oh! But how can I do that if you don't know the steps?"

"My friends from school will help!" said

Harrison eagerly. "I'll go and get them!"
He darted off.

"Do you really think this will work?"
Nori asked the girls excitedly.

Jasmine's hazel eyes sparkled. "I'm sure
it will. Besides, we have to try!"

Harrison returned with two school
friends. "This is Emery," he said, dragging
forward a boy elf who had spiky dark
hair and was
carrying a violin.
"And this is
Quigley."
Quigley was
a girl elf
with thick
red plaits,
freckles and very
pointed ears.

"I can play the tune for you," Emery said, holding up his violin.

"And I can show you the dance," Quigley offered.

"That would be wonderful!" said Jasmine. "Then hopefully I can teach Harrison."

"We'll help you!" said Quigley.

Emery took his violin out of its case and started to play a lively tune. Quigley performed the dance once all the way through and then did it more slowly so Jasmine could work out the steps. It was complicated, but Jasmine had had lots of dance lessons, so she picked it up easily.

"OK, so it starts with a step to the side then a spin and a jump and three steps back," Jasmine told Harrison. She showed him what she meant.

Harrison tried to copy but stumbled over his feet and almost fell over. He picked himself up and then tried again, but now he couldn't remember the steps.

Quigley went on one side of him and Jasmine on the other and they tried to guide him through it.

Ellie turned to Summer. "I think it might take him a little while to learn the whole dance. Shall we go and find Trixi or King Merry and see if there's anything we can do to help the fallen stars while we're waiting?"

Summer nodded and, leaving Jasmine and Quigley patiently explaining the steps to Harrison, they set off to find Trixi.

The hall was filling up now. The flying horses and dream dragons seemed to be

doing a great job of bringing the fallen
stars to Starshine Manor. The room was
full of glowing horse-shaped and dragon-
shaped stars. As the elves and pixies
began to treat them, the stars changed
and took the form of the elves and pixies.
But whatever form they were in, they all
looked weak and sad.

Summer spotted Trixi on her leaf. "Are you OK, Trixi?"

The little pixie's hair was even messier than usual and she looked flustered, but she still managed a smile. "Oh, there's so much to do! I can't stop. We've still got a few fallen stars out in the kingdom that need rescuing. I need to check on the stars in here, but I've also got to find King Merry."

"Can we help you?" Ellie asked.

"Oh, yes please!" Trixi gave her a relieved look. "That would be wonderful."

"I can look at the map to see how many stars are left and send out the horses and dragons," said Ellie.

"And I can check how the stars here are doing," said Summer.

"Where's Jasmine?" Trixi said, looking round.

"She's working on a way to break Queen Malice's spell," said Ellie.

Trixi beamed. "Oh, that's fantastic! I'll go and tell King Merry what's going on. Thank you!"

She zoomed away. Ellie gave Summer a grin. "Looks like we've got work to do!"

Summer started helping the pixies, brownies and elves as they looked after the stars in all their different forms. She tucked blankets around them and comforted them. Meanwhile, Ellie went

over to the map. There were still five stars shining on the map who needed to be found. One was at Clearsplash Waterfall, two were up on the mountainous slopes around Jewel Cavern and the remaining two were in Unicorn Valley.

"We'll go and fetch the stars by Jewel Cavern," volunteered two of the fairies.

"And I'll fetch the two in Unicorn Valley," offered Swift the flying horse.

"Great! Thank you so much," said Ellie. "But watch out for Queen Malice and her Storm Sprites!"

As the horse flew off, Ellie looked back at the map. There was just one star left now, but it was all the way at Clearsplash Waterfall, a long way away.

"Ellie!" rumbled a gentle voice. She turned and saw a dream dragon with

shimmering pink-and-cream scales
coming out of the hall.

"Pan!" Ellie said in delight. The
beautiful dragon nudged Ellie with her
huge head.

She didn't have wings — dream dragons
simply galloped through the air when
they flew. Usually they scattered dream
dust around the kingdom, which sent
everyone to sleep each night and gave

them lovely dreams, but tonight they were busy helping King Merry. No one in the kingdom wanted to sleep while the stars were missing from the sky.

"It's good to see you," said Pan, gazing down at her through her long eyelashes.

"And you," Ellie told the dragon. "There's just one star left to get. It's far away, though – by Clearsplash Waterfall."

"I can go and fetch it," said Pan. "I'll fly as fast as the wind."

Ellie smiled. "Thank you!"

Pan nuzzled her. "Would you like to come with me?"

Ellie shook her head. "No thanks, Pan!" she giggled. She hated heights, and although the big dragon had made her feel safe last time they'd flown together, Ellie only flew when she really had to.

"If you don't mind, I'll stay with my feet on the ground!"

Pan nodded. "I shall go on my own then. I'll see you when I get back."

"Good luck," Ellie called as Pan galloped up into the sky and flew away.

Now that Pan had gone to fetch the last star, Ellie headed back towards the observatory. *How is Jasmine getting on?* she wondered. *I hope Harrison's getting the hang of it!*

She peeked into the room where Jasmine was teaching the little elf the steps. As Ellie watched, Harrison tripped and fell over again. Ellie's heart sank. Oh dear, it didn't look like the dancing lesson was going very well at all!

# Breaking the Spell

As Ellie reached them, Jasmine helped Harrison back to his feet.

"I told you I was useless," Harrison said forlornly.

"No, you're not, we can do this," Jasmine told him patiently. "Now just try that step again. It's step, hop, turn." She bounced across the floor gracefully.

Quigley was sitting watching with Emery, who was having a rest from playing the violin. "You can do it!" they told their friend. "Keep trying."

Summer came over. "How's it going?"

Jasmine pulled her and Ellie to one side. "Not well," she whispered. "He gets so worried trying to remember what steps come next that he gets his feet all tangled up. He keeps falling over!"

"Magic!" said Ellie suddenly. "Maybe we could get Trixi to help in some way. She could enchant his feet or...or..."

"Magic dancing shoes!" gasped Jasmine, remembering when she'd had stage fright once and her friends had helped her. "Trixi might be able to conjure up some shoes that would magically help him dance really well."

"Brilliant idea!" said Summer. "You keep practising with Harrison, Ellie and I will find Trixi."

They found Trixi in the hall, talking to one of the flying horses, and she followed them back to the observatory. "What's going on?" she asked when they arrived.

Jasmine explained her idea.

Harrison's eyes lit up. "Magic dancing shoes! They sound amazing! I bet even *I* could dance with magic shoes."

Trixi considered it. "I suppose I could try and conjure up some shoes that can dance really well, although spells like this are never very reliable."

"We don't know what else to do," sighed Ellie.

"OK, let me think of a spell…" said Trixi. A frown creased her tiny forehead.

"Got it!" she declared. "What shoe size are your feet, Harrison?"

"Elf size three," he replied.

Trixi tapped her ring and called out:

*"Shoes that dance, in elf size three,
I need you now, please come to me!"*

There was a bright green flash and suddenly there on the ground in front of Trixi was a pair of sparkling silver shoes. As the girls watched, the shoes did a little tap dance all on their own.

"Will they work?" Harrison asked, his eyes wide. "Will I really be able to dance if I wear them?"

"Only one way to find out!" said Jasmine excitedly. "Try them on."

The shoes danced to one side, then

another. Harrison ran after them, trying
to grab them but they kept leaping out of
his reach.

"They seem a bit naughty," Summer
whispered to Ellie and Jasmine.

"Got you!" Harrison gasped, diving on
top of the shoes and holding them down.
He sat on them while he
pulled his elf boots
off and then he put
the new shoes on.
"They're great,"
he said, starting to
stand up.

The shoes
immediately started to
do a lively tap dance.
Harrison's arms windmilled
round and he fell to the

ground again. "Whoa!" he said, lying on his back. The shoes kept dancing even when his feet were sticking up in the air.

"Stop it, shoes!" Trixi said crossly.

The shoes stopped. But as soon as Harrison put his feet on the floor they started tap-dancing again. Harrison tried to stand up but the shoes were moving too fast. He scrabbled round on the floor on his hands and knees, his feet tapping with a life of their own.

"Oh dear, that didn't work," said Jasmine. "Take the shoes off, Harrison. It's no good if they just do the dance they want to do and not the dance you need."

Trixi sighed. "I'm sorry. It's a really difficult kind of magic and it's been such a busy day and night." She rubbed her eyes wearily and gave a tiny yawn.

Jasmine knew she couldn't ask the little
pixie to try and do any more magic.
"Don't worry, we'll keep trying the non-
magical way," she said. "We'll manage,
I'm sure. We *have* to grant this wish."

The little elf sadly took the shoes off
and Trixi tapped her pixie ring, making
them vanish with a popping sound.
Jasmine and Ellie helped Harrison up.

"Maybe it would help if Summer and I
danced with you?" Ellie suggested.

"OK." Harrison agreed.

Jasmine started trying to teach all of
them the dance. But Summer was almost
as bad at dancing as Harrison and they
both kept bumping into each other and
getting the giggles!

"This isn't working!" sighed Jasmine.

Summer felt bad for laughing when

Jasmine was trying so hard. She thought about how she could help. "I know!" she said, suddenly having an idea. "Do you like stories, Harrison?"

"Oooh yes," Harrison said eagerly.

"Well, how about I try turning the dance into a story to see if that helps you remember it?" said Summer. "What do you think, Jasmine?"

Jasmine shrugged. "It's worth a shot!" She'd try anything!

"Show me the whole dance," said Summer, thoughtfully.

Jasmine danced it all the way through and Summer put a story together in her head. "OK, Harrison, imagine that you're a baby duckling. The dance starts when you pop out of the reeds in the morning, you jump to one side and then the other,

looking round, checking if any of your
friends are there. Then you spin round
and give a little shake of your tail." She
tried not to giggle as she did a shimmy
– the movement did look quite like a
duckling shaking its tail feathers.

Ellie could see what Summer was

doing. "After that, the duck takes a big
jump out into the water and spins around
because the water is so cold."

"Can I have a go?" asked Harrison eagerly. "I think I can remember that."

Step by step, the three of them coached Harrison through the dance until he could do all the moves.

"There we are," Ellie said. "Now you can do the whole dance. Let's start the music and you can do it all, right from the beginning."

Harrison looked anxious. "I'm never going to remember it all!"

Summer took his hand. "You can do it," she told him. "Just think about the story."

Jasmine looked round to where Emery was watching with Quigley. "Would you play the music again, please?" Jasmine asked him.

"Of course!" Harrison's friend jumped to his feet and began to play.

The girls crossed their fingers tightly as Harrison began. "I'm a little duck," he mumbled as he remembered the beginning.

Summer, Jasmine and Ellie held their breath as he did a perfect shimmy before the big leap then spun round just as Jasmine had taught him. He wasn't getting a single step wrong!

As he clapped his hands and twirled again, Ellie noticed a slight commotion downstairs. She peered down the spiral

staircase and saw Pan coming in through the door with a fallen star in the shape of a weakly-glowing dream dragon.

"It's Pan with the last fallen star!" Ellie whispered, not wanting to distract Harrison when he was doing so well.

"All the stars are safe!" rumbled Pan.

Everyone downstairs cheered.

Summer glanced at her friends. "But we still have to break Queen Malice's spell and get them back into the sky!"

"Come on, Harrison," urged Jasmine. "Just a few more steps to go!"

The elf spun and twirled and shimmied and ended with a final leap.

"I did it!" he cried in delight. "I've learned the steps and I'll be able to do them at the school dance! My wish has come true!"

A loud cracking noise sounded – and suddenly all the stars started to glow and shine! They look round at each other in wonder, then began to change back into their star forms.

"Queen Malice's spell has broken!" cried Ellie.

"We can fly!" cried Morna. "We'll be able to grant wishes after all!"

"Wheeeee!" cried Eve, thrilled that her friends had got their magic back. She turned into her star form and shot up to the ceiling.

All around the hall, the other stars transformed too. It was like being surrounded by fireworks going off as they whizzed up to the ceiling and flew around, sparkling brightly.

"Wheee! Wheee! Wheeeee!"

Jasmine, Ellie and Summer
hugged each other.

"Oh, well done, my friends!" cried King
Merry, clapping his hands together in
delight and dancing on the spot. "You've
done it! You've saved the day again."

All the elves, pixies and brownies
cheered and the horses whinnied.

CRACK!

A thunderclap rocked the room

and the cheers turned to screams as
Queen Malice suddenly appeared in the
entrance to the hall. Her Storm Sprites
flapped around behind her.

"Not so fast!" she yelled, pointing her
tall, new staff into the room with its
spiky, golden thunderbolt on top. "You
have not beaten me yet, oh no!" Her eyes
were as cold and hard as ice. "I still have
one more trick up my sleeve!"

# The Wicked Spell

Queen Malice glared at the frightened crowd nastily.

"Wheeee!" cried the stars. They flew down from the ceiling and started whizzing around Queen Malice's head in a glittering cloud.

"Leave me alone, you horrible sparkly creatures!" she screeched indignantly, flapping her arms as though the beautiful stars were a swarm of wasps. The stars flew out of her way before she could hit them.

Queen Malice stamped her foot angrily. "Enough! And now, since you tried to defeat me, I'm going to make the skies dark forever." She gave an evil cackle and pointed her thunder staff at the sky above her.

"What's she going to do?" Summer said anxiously.

"Whatever it is, it's definitely not going to be something good," Jasmine said.

Queen Malice screamed out a spell at the sky above:

"Darkness now shall rule the sky,
These stars will be too scared to fly!"

Suddenly, the stars stopped whizzing round her head and fell to the floor, landing with little bumps. They transformed back into all different shapes – elves, pixies, humans, dragons, horses – and huddled together sadly.

"We were up in the air. It was so frightening," an elf-shaped star sniffed.

"I'm never flying again," another sobbed miserably.

"What have you done now, sister?" King Merry cried in horror, hurrying outside as Queen Malice started to float away on a thunder cloud. Everyone else ran outside too.

Queen Malice cackled. "Enjoy the dark nights from now on, brother! Think of it as a punishment for daring to try to take away my magic!" She clapped her hands and her thundercloud carried her off, with her Storm Sprites flapping beside her. The sound of her triumphant laughter echoed back across the grounds towards them.

Jasmine, Ellie and Summer raced

outside to comfort the king.

"Oh, thrones and tiaras," he said in dismay, looking at the stars sobbing on the floor. "This is dreadful. Look at all the stars. They're so sad again."

"And frightened," said Trixi, flying round in circles on her leaf. "What are we going to do?"

"Please don't be scared of flying," Jasmine said, running over to Morna, who was with Eve and Nori nearby. "You loved flying before Queen Malice cast her spell. Can't you try and fly again – just a little way up into the air?"

"N…no," stammered Eve, shaking her head. "It's too frightening."

"I don't want to leave the ground," sniffed Morna.

"What if we fall?" said Nori.

"You won't, you'll be fine," Jasmine said.
But the stars didn't look convinced.

Pan came over with the other two
dream dragons – Chi and Huang.
"Queen Malice stopped us flying once,"
Pan rumbled. "She made us scared of the
dark so we wouldn't fly at night. But we
learned that there's nothing to be afraid

of. Please try and fly, beautiful stars."

"It's so much fun," said Chi, a white-and-silver dragon.

Huang, a purple dragon, nodded. "You swoop and soar and…"

"Noooo," moaned the stars covering their ears. "Don't say any more."

Jasmine bit her lip. This wasn't getting them anywhere.

"It's just too scary to think about going into the sky," said Nori, tears welling up in her eyes.

Ellie nodded. "I understand. I'm scared of heights, you see, and I don't like flying much. But I've done it lots of times because I've had to when we've been trying to stop Queen Malice. Sometimes you have to do things that scare you."

"Ellie's right," said Summer. "I've swum

underwater and dived and I'm scared of
both those things but I had to do them
and my friends helped me. With the help
of your friends, you can do anything."

Jasmine joined in. "Won't you let us
help you? We can't let Queen Malice
win. We have to get you back up into the
night sky."

Eve, Morna and Nori looked at each

other determinedly.

"The girls are right," Eve said to her cousins. "We have to be brave."

"We must fly into the sky and sparkle," agreed Nori.

"No matter how frightening it is," said Morna with a gulp.

"We shall do it!" Eve said. She stood up and led everyone outside. Ellie took hold of Eve's hands, Summer took Nori's, and then Morna and Jasmine joined hands too. The other stars, together with all the brownies, elves and pixies, gathered around in a big group to watch them.

Eve looked at Ellie. Ellie's tummy tingled. She didn't really want to fly but she knew they had to do it. She remembered what Summer had said and lifted her chin bravely.

"Fly, stars, fly!" Jasmine exclaimed.

Gripping Ellie's hands tightly, Eve shot into the air. Ellie screwed her eyes shut as her feet left the ground. They were going higher and higher, she could feel it. Nearby, Summer and Nori rose into the air. Next, Morna and Jasmine flew into the sky. The other stars, seeing their friends soar into the sky, suddenly realised that there was nothing to fear. One by

one, they left the ground…

CRACK!

With a loud thunderclap, Queen
Malice's wicked spell broke. The last
star was flying! Instead of there being a
frightened silence, the sky was now filled
with shouting and laughing. Ellie heard
Summer and Jasmine whoop beside her.

"Open your eyes, Ellie!" Jasmine cried.

Ellie forced her eyes open. "Oh, wow!"

she gasped in amazement.

All the stars apart from Nori, Morna and Eve had transformed back into their star shapes and the night was filled with sparkling shooting stars, rushing into the sky with light streaming out behind them.

Holding hands high above the Secret Kingdom, Ellie and Eve danced around in a circle. Far below, Ellie could see lights come on in Wildflower Wood and Fancy Dress Village, in Dream Dale, the Enchanted Palace and at the Sugarsweet Bakery. The whole of the land seemed to be twinkling and the sky around her was glowing with stardust.

A furious shriek echoed faintly through the air. Ellie looked round and saw Queen Malice on her thundercloud, flying towards Thunder Castle.

"Nooooooo!" the queen screamed. "You pesky girls!" Bolts of lightning whizzed from her staff, firing into the night, but the stars easily avoided them.

"We've done it!" cried Ellie in delight. "We really have beaten Queen Malice!"

# Wishing Magic

One by one, the stars shot off into the night sky, until Ellie, Summer and Jasmine were just left with Eve, Nori and Morna. Each pair danced round in a circle in the starry sky. It was wonderful to see the whole of the Secret Kingdom laid out below them.

"Let's fly higher!" cried Eve.

"Oh yes!" gasped Jasmine and Summer and even Ellie didn't object. She wanted

to swoop and twirl in the sky for as long
as she could. It was amazing!

They flew up among the other stars.
One shot past them and they dived after
it, racing through the sky with it before
it got away. Jasmine and Morna turned
a somersault together and Ellie and Eve
spun each other round.

"I never want to go down to the
ground again!" said Summer as she
and Nori shot upwards like rockets in a
fireworks display.

They stayed in the sky for ages,
swooping and twirling, surrounded by the
glittering, shooting stars. They zoomed
through the air so fast the girls' hair blew
back behind them and their laughter was
whisked from their mouths.

Finally they shot back towards

Starshine Manor, flying so low that they could see King Merry and Trixi waving and laughing.

Eventually the stars led them back down to the ground, holding tightly to the girls' hands. As they landed, all the brownies and elves surged forward, cheering, and the pixies and fairies flew loop the loops over their heads.

"Look at the sky!" cried Trixi.

The girls glanced up. From down on the ground they could see the stars shooting through the sky above. It was a beautiful sight.

"We have our wishing magic back," said Eve. "And it's all down to you." She smiled a sparkly smile at Jasmine, Summer and Ellie. "Thank you!"

"And now everyone here can make

their wishes," said Morna.

"You must wish too," Nori said to the girls. "When we reach the highest point we'll each grant a wish! Maybe it will be one of yours."

The stars bowed their heads to the girls. "We must go now," said Eve. "But whenever you look into the sky you will see us there." She turned to King Merry. "Goodbye, Your Majesty."

He smiled. "Go, my dears and shine brightly for everyone to see!"

Eve cried, "Wheeee!" as she shot into the sky in delight, then turned into her shimmering star form.

"Wheee! Wheeee!" Nori and Morna followed her. The girls watched them fly up high and join the other stars.

"I'm so glad they're back where they

belong," said Summer happily.

"And it's all thanks to the three of you,"
said King Merry. "Oh, my dear friends,
how lucky we are to have you!" He
smiled so broadly his glasses wobbled on
his nose. "And now, I think it's time for
everyone to begin to make some wishes!"

Some of the elves ran inside and
returned with the big tartan blankets
and cushions. They laid them out and
everyone crowded onto them, lying on
their backs to stare up into the starry sky.

King Merry lay back on a blanket and
wriggled to get comfy. "It's been a very
busy few days, but everything has turned
out well. Ahhhh. Now what shall I wish
for? Let me see…" He sighed happily and
shut his eyes.

"There's one!" Ellie spotted a star

streaking across the sky.

"And another!" Harrison squealed happily.

"Make your wishes, everyone!" called Trixi excitedly.

Ellie shut her eyes. *What did she really want?* She smiled as she realised and silently wished as hard as she could.

She glanced beside her and saw Jasmine

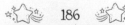

and Summer staring up at the sky, their lips moving slightly as they made their wishes too.

Ellie gasped as silver light suddenly surrounded her, making her skin and hair sparkle. Summer and Jasmine were shining too!

"Your wishes must have been granted!" exclaimed Trixi.

The girls sat up and looked at each other in delight.

"What did you wish for?" Summer asked Jasmine.

Jasmine smiled. "I wished we could keep coming to the Secret Kingdom for lots more adventures."

Summer and Ellie both clapped their hands to their mouths.

"That's what I wished for!" said Ellie.

"Me too!" said Summer.

They all burst out laughing.

As everyone exchanged happy grins, the last of the starlight faded out of the lantern in the observatory and the roof of the house grew dark.

"That's it," said Trixi flying down to the girls. "The Starlight Ceremony is finally over for another year."

The girls got to their feet. A loud snore rang out. They turned round saw that King Merry had fallen asleep on the blanket.

"Oh dear, poor King Merry's completely tired out," giggled Trixi.

Ellie yawned. "Me too."

"I think it's time you went home for now," said Trixi.

"Will you say goodbye to King Merry for us when he wakes up?" asked Jasmine, yawning too.

"And thank him for inviting us," said Summer. "It's been a wonderful adventure."

"Absolutely out of this world!" said

Ellie with a grin.

King Merry woke up with a snort, and the girls rushed round to hug him goodbye.

Trixi kissed them all on their noses.

"We'll be seeing you again very soon,"
she promised.

"Especially now my sister has her
magic back." King Merry shook his head
and sighed. "Who knows what she'll be
up to next?"

"Well, we'll be here to stop her!"
Jasmine grinned.

Everyone said goodbye. The dream
dragons nuzzled them and Harrison
gave them each a hug. Then Trixi tapped
her ring and a sparkling cloud of stars
surrounded the girls. They were lifted up
into the air. Just before they were whisked
away they saw Trixi tap her ring again
and King Merry was suddenly cuddled
up in a fleecy purple blanket with his
nightcap on his head.

"Good night, Secret Kingdom!" called

Jasmine as they were whisked away.

They landed back in the glade beside the shower block at the campsite.

Ellie shook her head. It was always a bit of a shock coming back to the real world. It felt so different from the Secret Kingdom. "What an adventure," she said.

"Look! The stars are back in the sky here too," said Summer.

Jasmine smiled. "Just think, a little while ago we were up there with them!"

They were silent for a moment as they remembered how amazing it had been to be up in the sky, swooping and dancing with the shooting stars.

"I'll never forget it," said Summer softly.

"Me neither." Jasmine squeezed Summer and Ellie's hands. "I'm glad the stars granted our wishes."

"And we'll have lots more adventures in the Secret Kingdom," said Ellie.

The girls looked up at the stars sparkling in the sky, lighting up both their world and the Secret Kingdom.

*More adventures*, thought Summer happily. She couldn't wait!

In the next Secret Kingdom adventure, Ellie, Summer and Jasmine meet the

# Candy Cove Pirates

**Read on for a sneak peek...**

## A Sweet Village

"These colouring books are great," said Ellie Macdonald, holding up one with a skull-and-crossbones flag on the cover.

"Connor's crazy about pirates," her friend Summer Hammond said with a smile. "He keeps making all his cuddly toys walk the plank!"

Connor was one of Summer's little brothers. His pirate-themed birthday party was tomorrow and he and Summer's youngest brother, Finn, could hardly wait for it to begin! Summer and her best friends, Ellie Macdonald and Jasmine Smith, were in Summer's bedroom putting party bags together.

"These eye patches are good, too," Jasmine said, putting one on. "Arr, shiver me timbers!"

Ellie laughed, making her red curls bob around her face. "All you need now is a wooden leg and you'd be a perfect pirate." She put the colouring book into the party bag she was filling.

"Look!" gasped Summer suddenly, pointing towards her wardrobe.

Ellie and Jasmine turned and saw that a silvery glow was shining out of the narrow gap between the wardrobe doors.

"The Magic Box!" Jasmine cried eagerly.

The three girls shared a wonderful secret. They looked after a wooden box carved with mermaids and unicorns and other fantastic creatures. But it wasn't just any box, it was a Magic Box! It could take them to an amazing land called the Secret Kingdom, where brownies, unicorns, pixies and other magical creatures lived, ruled by kind King Merry. The girls had visited lots of times to help solve the problems caused by Queen Malice, the king's horrid sister, who was always trying to take over her brother's kingdom, and make everyone in it miserable.

Summer threw open her wardrobe and took out the wooden box. The mirror on the lid was shining with light.

"I hope Queen Malice isn't causing trouble again," Ellie said anxiously.

"If she is, we'll soon stop her," Jasmine said determinedly.

Summer put the box on her bed and they all gathered round. She held her breath as a riddle appeared in the mirror and Ellie read it out:

"Dear friends, please come to somewhere sweet,
To share a Secret Kingdom treat.
You'll find this village near the sea,
Just call its name to summon me!"

The box lid flew open and a sheet of paper floated out. It was a map of the Secret Kingdom with tiny figures moving across it. "Look at the unicorns," said

Summer, pointing to three creatures galloping through a green valley, their colourful tails streaming out behind them.

"Let's look along the coast," Jasmine said. "Remember, we're searching for a village... somewhere sweet... "

"Fancy Dress Village, where everyone dressed up in those amazing costumes, was full of sweet little cottages," said Summer thoughtfully, "but it wasn't near the sea."

"There!" Jasmine cried. "That village is next to the water and it's called Candy Cove! That sounds really sweet."

"It must be the place," agreed Ellie.

The girls exchanged excited looks. "The answer is Candy Cove!" they cried together.

There was a brilliant flash of pink

light, then gold–and–silver sparkles came whooshing out of the box and whirled round Summer's bedroom. As the sparkles slowed, the girls saw a beautiful pixie with messy blonde hair riding on a leaf. "Trixi!" they exclaimed.

"It's so lovely to see you again," Trixi cried, beaming at them. She zoomed up to each of the girls and kissed them on the very tips of their noses.

"It's great to see you too, Trixi," said Summer happily.

"What a gorgeous outfit, Trixi," said Ellie. The little pixie was wearing a pink-and-white striped dress dotted with tiny candy canes. Her hat and shoes were pink, too, and they were scattered with multi-coloured sprinkles that reminded Ellie of hundreds and thousands.

"Thank you." Trixi twirled round on her leaf. "Are you ready for another trip to the Secret Kingdom?"

"You bet!" cried Jasmine.

"Has Queen Malice done something?" Summer asked anxiously.

"Not this time, thank goodness," Trixi said. "King Merry and I just wanted you to meet Mrs Sherbet."

"Who is she?" asked Ellie.

"She's in charge of the Secret Kingdom Sweet Shop," explained Trixi with a smile. "One of the kingdom's most delicious traditions!"

Jasmine licked her lips. This was all sounding very exciting!

"The Sweet Shop only appears once a year, in summer, and then Mrs Sherbet travels all around the kingdom for a week, sharing treats with everyone," continued Trixi. "It looks different every time. Last year it was shaped like a giant hot-air balloon and this year it's a magnificent ship – The Sweet Princess! The whole ship is made from delicious things to eat!"

"I can't wait to see it," Jasmine said, grinning at Ellie and Summer.

"Let's go!" Trixi cried. "The ship can't set sail until King Merry and Mrs Sherbet perform the launch ceremony. It has to be held at precisely midday when the tide is at its very highest. That way the ship has a brilliant start on its journey around the Secret Kingdom, taking a year's worth of sweets to everyone!"

Hurriedly the girls held hands. Trixi tapped her pixie ring and chanted:

"Take us as quickly as can be,
To Candy Cove beside the sea!"

A sparkling whirlwind whooshed out
of the Magic Box and lifted the girls
off their feet. It smelled of toffee and
humbugs, making their mouths water.

"Wheee!" cried Summer. "Secret
Kingdom, here we come!"

A moment later they landed with a
gentle bump in a old-fashioned little
village. The street was lined with cute
shops and workshops with red-and-
white striped awnings, and cottages with
thatched roofs and brightly coloured
front doors.

"Let's look at the workshops while we
wait for King Merry to arrive," suggested
Trixi. "All of Mrs Sherbet's sweet treats

are made in Candy Cove, then they are loaded on to the Sweet Princess, ready to be taken around the kingdom and be shared with everyone!"

Read
# Candy Cove Pirates
to find out what
happens next!

# Secret Kingdom

Collect all the amazing
Secret Kingdom specials - with
two exciting adventures in one!

# Spot the Difference

Queen Malice's Storm Sprites are causing trouble at the midnight feast! Can you spot five differences between the two pictures?

Picture two has only two star candles, an extra glass, no stripe on the elf's hat, a tiered cake instead of a jelly and no stars in the sky.

# Secret Kingdom

## Catch up on the very first books in the beautiful Secret Kingdom treasury!

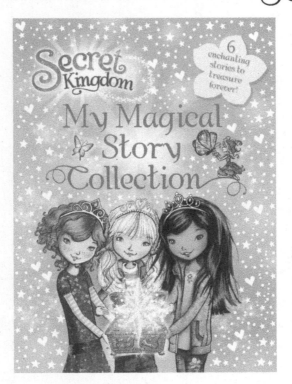

# Secret Kingdom

A magical world of
friendship and fun!

Join the Secret Kingdom Club at

# www.secretkingdombooks.com

and enjoy games, sneak peeks and lots more!

You'll find great activities, competitions, stories
and games, plus a special newsletter for
Secret Kingdom friends!